Go For It, Ruby!

For Bella
JE

For my gorgeous Mr lols – love Mummy x
RH

First published 2009 by Macmillan Children's Books
a division of Macmillan Publishers Limited
20 New Wharf Road, London N1 9RR
Basingstoke and Oxford
Associated companies throughout the world
www.panmacmillan.com

ISBN: 978-1-4050-5191-0 (hb)
ISBN: 978-0-230-70738-2 (pb)

Text copyright © Jonathan Emmett 2009
Illustrations copyright © Rebecca Harry 2009
Moral rights asserted.
You can find out more about Jonathan Emmett's books at
www.scribblestreet.co.uk

1 3 5 7 9 8 6 4 2

A CIP catalogue record for this book is available from the British Library.

Printed in China

Written by
Jonathan Emmett

Illustrated by
Rebecca Harry

MACMILLAN CHILDREN'S BOOKS

Once upon a time,
upon a nest,
beside a lake,
there lived a family of ducks.

A mother duck,
a father duck and
five young ducklings.

The smallest duckling was called Ruby.
And while her brothers and sisters were
always in a hurry, Ruby took things slowly,
in her own time.

One afternoon, Ruby was exploring the edge of
the lake when she spotted Errol, a young gosling,
struggling among the reeds.

"Fluff and feathers!" cried Errol. "I'm stuck!"
"Would you like some help?" asked Ruby.
"Yes please!" said Errol.

Ruby carefully pushed back the stems and Errol wriggled free.
"What were you doing?" asked Ruby.
"I'm trying to find the **Golden Pool**," said Errol.

Ruby gasped! She had heard stories of
the Golden Pool. It was a mysterious place,
hidden somewhere near the lake.

"Why do you think the pool is here?" she whispered.
"Because I've searched everywhere else!" said Errol.

"I just have to get through these reeds," grunted Errol, charging back into the stems.

"Are you sure that's the best way?" asked Ruby.
"What other way is there?" asked Errol.
"Sometimes," explained Ruby, "it's best to stop and think.
Let me show you."

Errol followed Ruby as she swam
slowly through the winding reeds,
looking carefully around her.

"There!" she said, as a
fat fish swam across their path.
"He seems to know his way around.
Let's follow him!"

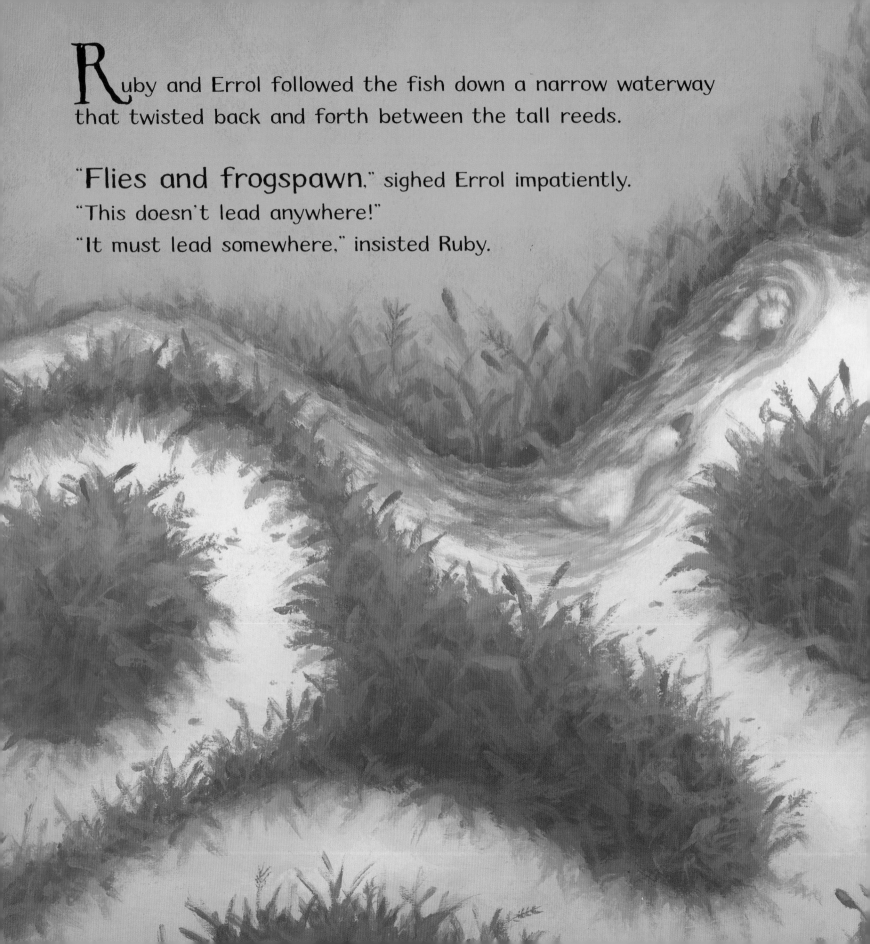

Ruby and Errol followed the fish down a narrow waterway that twisted back and forth between the tall reeds.

"Flies and frogspawn," sighed Errol impatiently.
"This doesn't lead anywhere!"
"It must lead somewhere," insisted Ruby.

But just as Ruby was beginning
to think Errol might be right . . .

. . . the waterway opened out into a wide pool,
roofed with blossom-filled branches.
Slim shafts of sunlight cast beautiful patterns
onto the surface of the water.

They had found
the **Golden Pool**.

"Beaks and bills!" cried Errol,
darting out into the middle.
"We found it!
We found it!"

Ruby followed after him – slowly and quietly.
It was the most beautiful place she'd ever been.

But then she spotted something odd!
A scattering of blossom fell upon the water, drifted
quickly across the surface, then **vanished**
at the far side of the pool!

What happened there? Ruby wondered,
swimming over to take a closer look.

By the time she saw the waterfall,
it was almost too late!

"Stop!" cried Ruby, as Errol darted past her. "It's a **waterfall!** If we get too close, we'll be swept over the edge."

But they were already too close. And the water was moving
so fast that, no matter how hard the two friends paddled,
they could not get away.

"What are we going to do?" cried Ruby.

Just then a long branch floated past.
"Quick!" called Errol. "Hold onto it!"

Without thinking, Ruby followed Errol and grabbed hold of the branch as it swept towards the edge of the waterfall . . .

At the last moment, the branch caught on the bank and Ruby and Errol scrambled to safety.

"That was **brilliant!**" gasped Ruby. "How did you
know the branch would get caught like that?"
"I didn't," said Errol. "I just hoped it would."

"Sometimes," said Errol, "it's best to stop and think.
But sometimes, you just have to **go for it!**"

The two friends decided it was safer to
walk back as far as they could.

"Fluff and feathers!" said Ruby,
when the bank eventually ran out.
"It looks like we'll have to swim the last bit!"

Errol smiled. "Are you sure?" he said.
"Sometimes, it's best to stop and think."

But Ruby had
already jumped in
and was paddling home.

"And sometimes," she called back to him, "you just have to GO FOR IT!"